The LION OF St ANDREWS

Published in Great Britain
by SERAFINA PRESS
The Smokehouse Gallery
St Ella's Place
Eyemouth
Berwickshire
TD14 5HP
www.serafinapress.co.uk
www.lionofstandrews.com

ISBN 978-0-9572309-0-3

First published in Great Britain in 2012

Printed in Great Britain by Martins the Printers,
Berwick upon Tweed
www.martins-the-printers.com

For Maureen and Hugh O'Neill
and
Fiona Turnbull; lion-hearts all.

And for their grandchildren;
Aidan and Michael, Abbie and Lewis.

J.T.D.

For Liam and Dad;
the ever-patient men in my life.

K.C.

THE LION OF ST ANDREWS

Written By

Jennifer T. Doherty

Illustrated by

Katherine Coulton

One summer afternoon, as the sun warmed the white waves round
the sands at St Andrews...

...a boy called James sat on the steps by the harbour.

He was sleepy, half-listening to his parents and their friends nearby. They were talking to each other, but it was not very interesting talk.

James was bored. His parents had brought him to live in St Andrews, and he didn't have any friends yet.

He ran his fingers over the lines in the old stone wall, making little grains of sand fall out.

As he drowsed, he felt the wall beside him become warm, then warmer still. The stone seemed to move beneath his fingers.

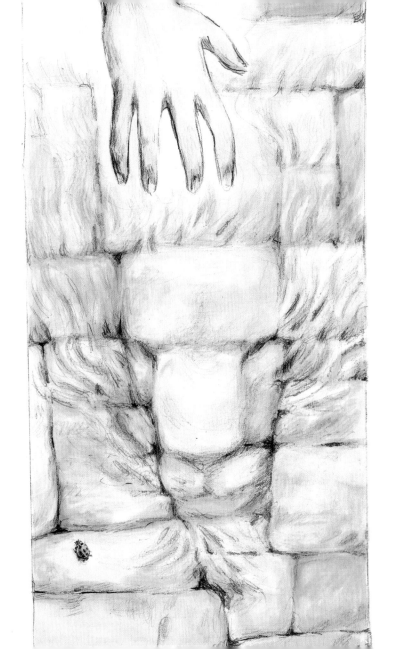

Gradually, a face began to appear. Out and out it pushed, until the whole head was visible. James jumped back, astonished.

What on earth was in this wall?

Then he heard music – quiet, but sharp and clear, and different from anything he had heard before.

As he listened, a lion stepped right out of the stone.

It was small, but quite definitely a lion – from its forepaws to its splendid tufted tail.

The lion sneezed and shook
its mane.

"Dusty in there," it said.
"Cosy enough. Still, time to
come out."

It held up a paw. "Don't be
frightened, young James. I'm
not going to harm you."

"How do you know
my name?"

"I'll tell you that later. These walls are very special. I'm not the only creature in there. Have you noticed anything else unusual?"

"Not really…" said James.

"Ah – I will show you! And you must see the old town. Come on." James stood up.

Would his parents notice the animal beside him?

"I'm off for a walk. Back in ten minutes," he called, and his parents waved. They didn't seem to have spotted the lion.

"Grown-ups!" he thought. "Always so busy with their own stuff."

When he turned around, he got a surprise. In just a few moments the lion had grown much larger.

"No one can see me unless I let them," said the lion. "And no one can see you as long as you are with me. Right – jump up."

James loved the feeling of riding high on the lion's back. They climbed the hill towards the cathedral. This was *definitely* the most fun he'd had since he came to St Andrews.

As they went through the gate leading to the town, everything seemed peculiar.

At first he thought it was a pageant or a fair, but then he realised that this was something very different.

The ruined cathedral was not a ruin any longer. Somehow, the buildings looked older, but newer. Everyone's clothes looked strange.

The whole town seemed to jostle and push, as crowds of people moved towards the magnificent, towering cathedral.

'It's a Procession Day," said the lion. "A great feast, calling in townspeople and pilgrims.

The pilgrims travel from all over the country. They even come from abroad to honour the bones - the relics of Saint Andrew – here in the cathedral."

"Look - you can tell the far-away pilgrims by their badges and the scallop shells on their hats. They come hoping for cures or miracles, so they make a special journey here," said the lion.

"Today it's warm, but pilgrims arrive here in winter too, and all through the year."

"So are we back in Long Ago?" asked James, slipping down from the lion's back.

"We are. I want you to understand this town where you're living. And to discover why yo[u] have come to St Andrews."

"I know why I've come! My parents brought me here."

"That's not what I mean," said the lion, as they padded closer to the cathedral, and stopped in front of the huge wall surrounding it.

"I want to show you something.

Just look. Look closely
at the wall."

James peered at the wall. At first, all he could see were plain stones. Slowly, slowly, he began to make out shapes.

He saw pictures of people...

catching fish

painting

feasting

singing

getting married

...all etched in the stone.

"How did they get there?" asked James.

The lion sat back on its haunches. "Whether they know it or not, everyone who arrives in St Andrews comes with a wish or a dream.

And people who live here carry hopes and longings too, of course."

"If a wish or a dream is important enough, it flies out of a person's heart, and comes to rest in the walls. When other people need to see it, they can."

They walked along further and they saw a baby in a shawl, a rose...

...and a beautiful harp.

James stopped short. "Oh, I like that harp!" he said.
"Me too," said the lion. "It sometimes comes out and plays for me. You might have heard it earlier. I knew the boy who dreamed it here.

His name was *James* - just like yours.

James was a poor boy who longed to play music. A family of harpists discovered his great skill, and offered him the chance to join them. He became one of the best-loved musicians in Scotland."

The lion looked at James. "Do you play music?"

"No..." James felt guilty – his parents had offered him lessons, but he had not wanted to learn.

Suddenly, James felt his hands ache to hold the harp.

He felt his fingers move, longing to pluck at the strings.

He wondered how long it took to become a real harpist.

'But I can't!" he thought.
'The other children would
laugh at me."

'Really?" he heard the lion
say, as though it had heard
him speak his fear aloud.

He looked at the lion, but it
stayed silent, as they gazed
for a few moments longer at
the images on the wall.

Then the lion said, "Right,
time to go back. Jump on
again."

As they left, James turned
to watch the last of the
procession. They moved
downhill towards the
harbour, until every sight
and sound of the old town
had disappeared.

James leaned forward and ruffled the lion's shaggy mane. "And you? How did you get here? And how did you know my name?"

"Long ago, a brave woman came to St Andrews. She came with the love of learning and a wish to share that love. Her courage and love created me. So I wait, in the stone, until it's time to meet someone who needs me. As I met you today, young James. I hear the hearts of those who choose to sit by me - that's how I knew your name."

They walked till they reached the harbour.
"Goodbye, my friend," said the lion, as James
jumped down.

In moments, the lion became small again, and vanished into the stone.
James found himself alone. The wall seeemed just a wall once more.

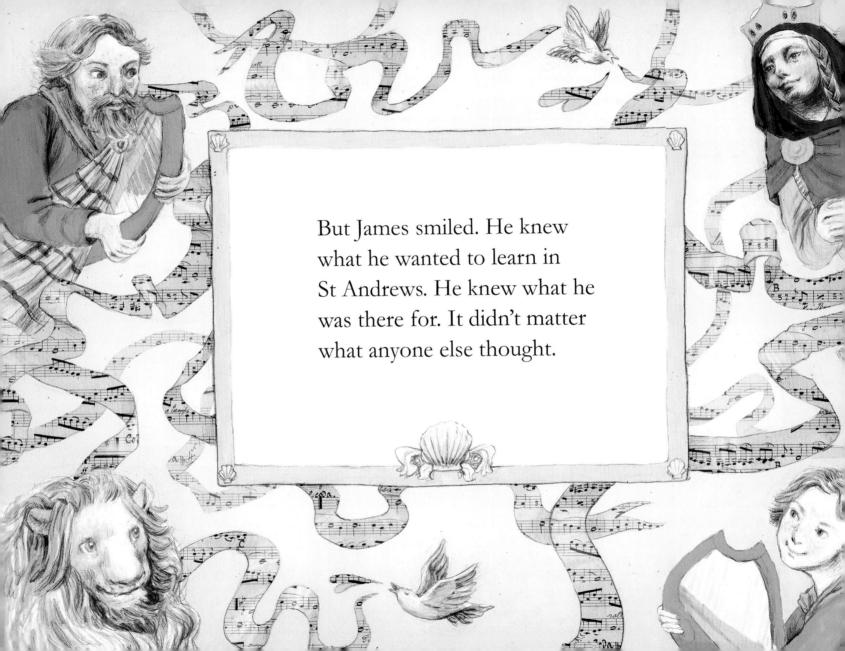

But James smiled. He knew
what he wanted to learn in
St Andrews. He knew what he
was there for. It didn't matter
what anyone else thought.

When he asked them,
James's parents said he
could have harp lessons.

His harp fast became
his most treasured
possession.

He made friends with a boy, Tom, who lived in his street.

For the rest of the holidays they spashed in the sea...

...raced along the beaches...

...explored the cathedral ruins.

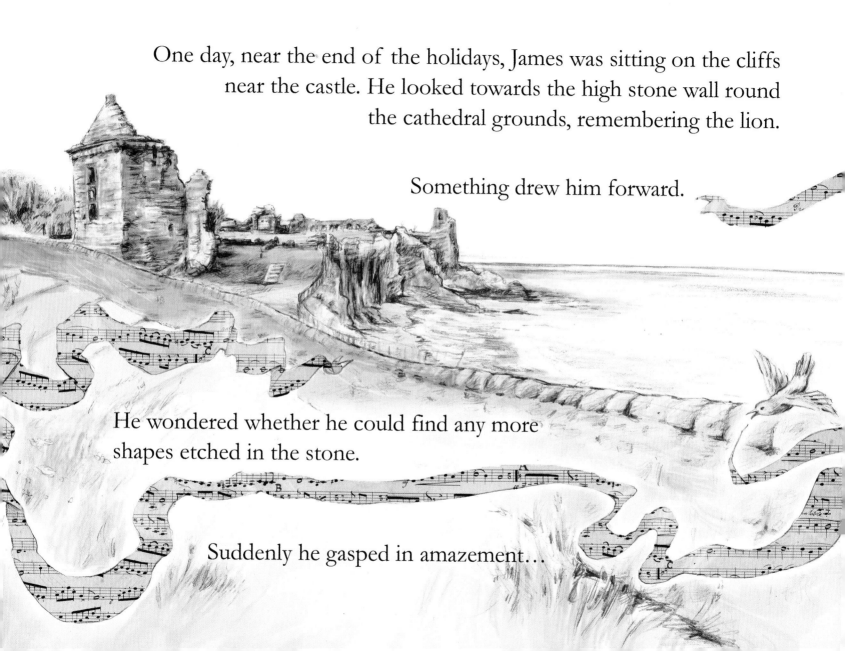

One day, near the end of the holidays, James was sitting on the cliffs near the castle. He looked towards the high stone wall round the cathedral grounds, remembering the lion.

Something drew him forward.

He wondered whether he could find any more shapes etched in the stone.

Suddenly he gasped in amazement...

Now, as though making music together, *two* splendid harps
rested in the wall.